FIRST STORY

First Story's vision is a society that encourages and supports young people from all backgrounds to practise creative writing for pleasure, self-expression and agency. We believe everyone has a unique voice, a story to tell and a right to be heard. Our flagship programme places inspiring professional writers into secondary schools, where they work intensively with students and teachers to develop young people's creativity, confidence and ability. Through our core provision and extended opportunities, including competitions and events, participants develop skills to thrive in education and beyond.

Find out more at firststory.org.uk

First Story is a registered charity number 1122939 and a private company limited by guarantee incorporated in England with number 06487410. First Story is a business name of First Story Limited.

First published 2023 by First Story Limited
44 Webber Street, Southbank, London, SE1 8QW

www.firststory.org.uk

ISBN 978-0-85748-568-7

1 3 5 7 9 10 8 6 4 2

A CIP catalogue record for this book is available from the British Library.

Printed and bound in the UK by Aquatint
Typeset by Avon DataSet Ltd
Copy-edited by Kirsten Irving
Proofread by Ingrid Wassenaar
Cover designed by Jennifer Hines (www.jenniferhines.design)

The Open Window

An Anthology by the First Story Group
at Platanos College

EDITED BY CECILIA KNAPP | 2023

FIRST STORY

Contents

Introduction

Cecilia Knapp, Writer-in-Residence

What a great year it has been at Platanos College, working with this group to express their lives, their experiences and their unique perspectives on the world. The group's enthusiasm, dedication and brilliance meant we worked really hard this year. They truly impressed me with their willingness to try things, to push language and imagery in impressive new ways, and to create new thought around a number of themes.

The anthology begins with poems of transformation – imagining a world in which we could be freer; a world that is more tolerant. At a time when compassion is increasingly lacking, it feels pertinent to begin this way, to give young people the opportunity to define and imagine their future on their own terms, sharing their own hopes for change. Poetry can change hearts and minds with a unique power that can cut right to our centres. This book begins with an invitation to look beyond what we know and aspire to a better future. From there, we move on to a series of poignant depictions of emotion; these poets find the language for complex feelings and show generosity in the ways they express them, allowing the reader to feel them too. They carve out space for joy and appreciation – from their friends and families, to odes to their bodies – as well as reflecting on the memories and experiences that have shaped them.

In the second section, 'Our People', we are privileged to learn about the people they value, their communities. We are invited into worlds that are not our own, in order to understand what is different there – and, of course, to see what we have in common. This section also draws upon invented characters and worlds built by these young writers as comments on society.

Lastly, we celebrate all the amazing places these young people love – from London's busy streets to the heat of Côte d'Ivoire to summertime in Morocco, shaded by a parasol. This section of the book is replete with smells, tastes, textures, colours and climates. These poems celebrate the ways in which places shape and inform our identities; they teach and share and celebrate the diversity of our city, and of Platanos College. These poems are teleporters, time machines and homes of different kinds – some comforting and some complicated.

One of my favourite sessions with the students this year was a session in which we read the poem 'Finding Space' by Jason Allen-Paisant, a poem that explores what it means to take up space as a member of a marginalised community. The students from Platanos engaged with the poem with empathy, and many really identified with the subject, writing their own depictions of claiming joy in public.

Further thanks must go to the following poets, who inspired much of the students' writing:

Polarbear (aka Steven Camden) and his poem 'Heartburn', Malika Booker's 'Brixton Market' and 'The House on Jubilee Street', Momtaza Mehri's 'Glory Be to the Gang Gang Gang', Fathima Zahra's 'Ode to My Thighs', Mary Ruefle's 'Japanese Bloodgod', Simon Armitage's 'Not the Furniture Game' and Sinéad O'Reilly's 'The Party'.

And of course, thank you so much to every single student who filled my Wednesday afternoons with laughter, thoughtful discussion, beautiful writing and double-stuffed Oreos. Thank you also to Godwin Hanson, Samantha Thompson and all of the staff at Platanos College who welcomed me so kindly, and who keep First Story thriving here. You work so hard for your students.

Teacher's Foreword

Godwin Hanson, Teacher of English

When asked to describe the act of writing, many would say it is challenging, strenuous and daunting – but this proved no problem for the pupils of Platanos College. Both cohorts took to writing with great aplomb. Ideas were lobbed across the room as we delved into an array of texts from week to week, before pupils were challenged to pick up a pen and adopt the role of the writer themselves.

Each week was a marvel to watch, as pupils devoured a range of texts and absorbed different creative techniques before generating their own poems: from using memoirs to recall past experiences to creating interesting characters with the help of a questionnaire, to retracing memories and focusing on their loved ones. Pupils were happy to draw on their varied experiences and cultures, and on their backgrounds, coming from countries like Côte d'Ivoire, Turkey and Nigeria. Pupils showed pride in their diverse cultures, and were deeply inspired by their families' experiences, using these as a basis upon which to form their own creative endeavours.

It was clear their creativity knew no bounds.

To describe our weekly meet-ups as mere sessions would not do justice to the enthusiasm and dedication of our pupils. Rather, they became melting-pots of culture, during which pupils felt free to express themselves, under the contagious enthusiasm of writer Cecilia Knapp. One of the most interesting things was seeing pupils morph into confident writers on a weekly basis, under Cecilia's guidance and expertise. Though initially nervous, the pupils – with motivational Oreos ever present – transformed into self-assured writers. Their statements soon changed from, 'I can't' to, 'Can I include this?' and, 'I can't believe I've written this!'

I leave you with these poems, stories and echoes of the past, present and future. From the creative hands, minds and imaginations of our pupils, welcome to *The Open Window*.

PART ONE

OURSELVES

All that we are, all that we feel, all that we can be

Free-Flight

Karina Ribeiro Sanches

If I were a bird, I would fly:
fly to see all I've missed as a person.
I would talk:
talk to learn the pattern in song.
I would sing:
sing to let all know my happiness.
I would live the life I do not have.
I would live knowing my purpose.
I would steal,
steal anything from anyone,
knowing it wouldn't affect me.

If I was a bird,
I would be a magpie:
bringing annoyance and joy alike.

My Muslim Life in Shakespearean Society

Ridwaan Isse

I have a dream that my people
will be looked at for their personality,
not their religion.
I wish that happened.
I'm not inferior to you.
I just want to fit in.
And don't even start,
I don't want to hear any part
of your hatred towards me,
towards us.
I have a dream
and one day, may this dream come true.

Stop Online Bullying

Israe Sehimi

Online bullying is bad
It can make people feel very sad
Please be careful who you are rude to
Because one day that could be you
You wouldn't like to be in their position
The hate could lead to an everlasting depression
So online bullying is very bad
It could make so many feel so sad
Please share this story

Anger

Hamza Ali

Anger is a busy head
Anxiety is scared intestines
Anger is a violent school

Sadness

Yahya Rodani

I throw it off a cliff but it crawls its way home
I feed it overcooked steak and burnt sandwiches while its
   stomach is growling
While people crumble at the thought of it, my mind stays
   impenetrable
I anaesthetise my sadness but it reawakens a few minutes later
I take my sadness to a graveyard, point at each tomb and
   threaten it with every word
As the days become weeks and the weeks become months
My impenetrable wall starts to corrupt
When months turn to years, I adapt to the relentless emotion
   infesting my mind

It Won't Last Forever

Princess Amosun

I obey my happiness
I protect my happiness
I spoil my happiness
I feed my happiness sweets, cake, pie
I love my happiness
I do everything and anything for it
Anything
But still
It spits on me
It mocks me
It leaves me
I beg for my happiness
Will it come back?

I Feed My Stress My Homework

Nesrin Osman

I feed my stress a chill pill
I throw my stress out of the window but it manages to bounce
    back
My stress knocks on the door and I reject it
I try to give my stress a friend but it always backfires
A good friend is what stress needs
But jealousy always bumps into it
Go away and don't come back
I've had enough
Cut me some slack

Apathy

Tiago Silva Jesus

I feel apathy
I feed it plain rice
I feed it gallons of water
I feed my apathy paper, trash, wood
The bounty on my apathy is big
I buy it paper to play with
I take it to the museum
I take it to visit friends in prison
I try to drown my apathy
I bite my apathy
I punch my apathy
But no matter what I do it will return
I live with it
I sleep with it
I am it

Boredom

Tiago Costa

I sit down on the ground with my boredom
I stare at the wall with my boredom
I eat Oreos with my boredom
I drink Fanta with my boredom
My boredom bounces like a tennis ball after a serve
I punch random stuff with my boredom
I go to the park with my boredom and kick a ball around

Bubblegum

Rosie Button

They meet me every day
They won't let go of my hand
They are my only friend
I just try to stay grand

Always next to me
Being very clingy
They need to know how I feel
Because it's a big deal

I'm stuck to them with bubblegum
They are always in my head
I'm stuck to them with bubblegum
They won't let me go to bed

I'm stuck to them with bubblegum
They are always in my head
I'm stuck to them with bubblegum
I can't believe what they said

Always calling me on my phone
They won't leave me alone
I just want to live my life
It's like I'm being stabbed with a knife

They just need to let me be
They need to realise I'm not happy
I just want to turn my back
Or put them under attack

I'm stuck to them with bubblegum
They are always in my head
I'm stuck to them with bubblegum
They won't let me go to bed

I'm stuck to them with bubblegum
They are always in my head
I'm stuck to them with bubblegum
I can't believe what they said

Heartbreak

Mariam Daud

Powerful heartbreak. It only happens once.
The pounding door of anger.
The unanswered questions.
Why did he leave you?
They don't tell you that loneliness is a bubble.
Depression is a bitter taste.
They don't tell you these things.
They tell you that
Love is the smell of roses.
Love is blissful.
But it really isn't.

Rosie

Rosie Button

The reddest rose
A beautiful flower
Red and bright
A ball rolling down a hill
My name
Is melting ice

My Name Is Israe

Israe Sehimi

I'm a Muslim
In the Quran it says my name
Some people call me Izzy
I do not mind it
I feel like my name is special
Because it's not common
I'm very happy about that
My name is the sky, paper, sand
And a see-saw
Excitement, happiness, joy

Felipe is Fun Like a Game

Felipe Silva

Felipe is a star in the solar system
Felipe is happiness
Happiness is loud hands
Happiness is a beating heart

Zayan

Zayan Miah

An old book in which I like to doodle
A delicious bowl of extravagant noodles
Playing football in competitions
My mum's pictures with flowers and my dad's car
When it rains on a pitch and you can slide with ease
When I learnt to swim in a pool, but it felt like the sea
Bangladesh's food and weather
Football, which will stay in my heart forever

Tiago

Tiago Costa

A mattress, soft to sleep on, where I spend most of my time
A delicately crispy chicken wing
A football flying through the sky, swiftly landing at my feet
A picture of me and Mum, saved on my phone
The summer, like a beam of light, beaming down happiness
The private park outside my old house
The sun shining down on the old people drinking beer at the
    Portuguese cafe

List of All That Brings Contentment

Karina Ribeiro Sanches

In praise of all that is sincere, call upon the rising of the sun; a sun on a perfect summer's morning, painting the sky with its beauty.

In the name of the mastered songs of many early birds, the two cats that patiently wait for their family's arrival after a long day of play. The playfights of two patient cats and friendliness after they have tired themselves.

The smell of the room that I come home to every day. The moment I fall asleep after trying to for hours. The silence and loneliness of a late, dark night.

Every time I return to the same friendly faces of my family.

Talking to friends who live far away. The excitement of a new release. The clank of 3D-printed plastic. Being alone at home, even if it is not truly alone. A full night's rest. An update to a story. Winning an argument.

And everything joyful in a world full of anger and hate.

Ode to My Hands

Nasir Anderson St Aubyn

If there were a choice of a million hands
I would still pick you
Even though you're very wobbly
And are bad at handwriting
You still help me everywhere, with everything
You have helped me to find the start of my life
And maybe you'll help me at the end of my life
I know you will be helping me
Every second, minute, hour of every day

In Praise Of

Jahmarlley Bollers

My mum's cooking
My sister's cooking
The gifts my family give me
The teachers who help me
Food shops
Money
My family
My friends
And fried chicken
And jerk chicken
And drinks
And Christmas trees
And the Bible
And the holidays

I Really Love My Eyes

Jahmarlley Bollers

But one thing I don't like is the colour
My eyes are brown/black
I want one to light up so I can see it in the mirror
But I'm grateful for the eyes I've got
Even though I don't like this colour
You need to be grateful for what you have
Anything can happen
Your wishes can come true

Appreciated

Indigo-Rose Egundebi

In praise of the beautiful sunset sky. In praise of life itself. In praise of all my loyal and trustworthy friends. In praise of my mum's delicious cooking. In praise of my family, always there for me, through the bad and good; how they look at me every time they see me all grown up. My mum: how she boosts me up with confidence, how she never lets me down. My little brother Theo, who brings out the fun side in me and my brother Ty-James. We may fight and argue but when we see each other down, we support each other. My sister Neyah, the best big sis of all time, and let's not forget my cheeky two-year-old rabbit and all of the other cheerful family in my life. These are the things and people that are appreciated in my life; the things and people that will always be appreciated.

Ode to My Body

Shelisha-Rayne Damsa

I don't know what I've done
but you know how to hold a grudge.
Still, you supply my food and allow me to breathe.
My eyes seem to only see false sides;
the flat waists, the long hair, the tall people
but when I blink I see the truth.
To my arms: you useless things,
that struggle to carry toilet roll,
but can carry the weight of desperation and sadness;
you allow me to write, to read.
To my legs:
I've seen turtles faster.
Can't run to save my life,
but you allow me to walk and play,
something do and need every day.
Most of all, to my brain:
you make me feel foolish for your stupid ideas,
but you help me get home, help me think and exist.
My body isn't perfect. My body isn't ideal.
It isn't much but it does so much for me.
It makes me
me.

I Remember

Stella Candido

I remember when I was four I had a dream.
The dream was about going to Hogwarts. (I really love Harry
    Potter.)
It was the first day and I got settled in Gryffindor.
I met Hermione Granger. Me and Hermione became best
    friends,
and later she introduced me to Harry and Ron.
After that we all became best friends.

Then I woke up, I was in the hospital.
I was so confused, then I remembered I was sick.
My mum was next to me, glad that I'd woken up.
My mum started telling me I'd almost recovered
and I was so happy.
A few hours later, me and my mum were talking
and my godmother walked in.
She brought me toy horses!
I was so happy I played with them straight away.

PART TWO

OUR PEOPLE

His Heart Is a Blossoming Flower

Tiago Silva Jesus

His eyes are the sparkling stars in the sky
His moustache is a ferret waiting to explore
His brain is a library of encyclopaedias
His mouth is an escalator
His feelings are a river of joy
His knees are a swing, rusting

My Dad at Work

Mariam Daud

I've never actually been there
But I can imagine him
Typing away on his laptop
With his glasses on the desk
His office neatly organised
But his table a mess
His kufi on
Typing a frustrated email to his boss
Him, thinking about what soup he wants
With his pounded yam
Him thinking about life
Him being him

My Sister

Yahya Rodani

Her nose is a quiet mouse in its house
Her brain is a fog of white
Her mouth is an endless parade of noise and music
Her eyes are a helpless ocean, waiting for...
Her heart is a hyena hunting its prey
Her knee is a fan spinning endlessly

My Little Bro

Princess Amosun

His hair was fresh-cut grass
His eyes were put-out flames
And his blink was a wave of destruction
His neck was a loose thread
His heart was a ripe apple
His arms were strong magnets
But his tears were a thousand unspoken words

My Memories

Maferima Bamba

I remember when I lost my mum
I had to look for her everywhere with my brother
We found a security guard to help us
Everyone started to crowd me
Eventually my mum found me
The security guard wasn't sure if it really was my mum
So he asked me and I was too shocked to speak
So my brother jumped in and said
This is my mum. Thank you for helping me find her
We left, me feeling traumatised
I realised that losing my mum was so scary
Imagine if I'd become an orphan!

Who Loves the Feeling

Zayan Miah

Of having a sleepover at your grandma's house?
Playing with your cousins, running around like a little mouse
Suddenly an amazing smell rushes to your nose
No need to think about where it's coming from; you already
    know
Eating my grandma's food is the best part of the day
Rushing to the kitchen to see what she's made
When I get thirsty I have some juice
Play with my baby cousin who's really cute
I never get bored; I have my cousins around me
Whenever I see them I'm always happy
Playing games on the bed, making dens with blankets
My grandma's house is the best place
I don't like it
I love it

Uncle J's Here

Shivani Clarke-Lewis

I'll never forget my uncle
Especially with the memories he left me
And even though I am sad that he is gone
I'm sure he is as happy as he can be
He was such a sweet man
A Manchester United stan
He will forever be in my heart
Whether it is super-bright or really dark
I can't forget his big, warm smile
And his comfy, cosy style
I loved his personality
The way he was always happy and full of glee
The way he made me laugh
So I hope he's looking down at me
Thinking, *I'm so proud of you Shivani*

Sweet, Sweet K

Faduma Adde

I can still see her flowers in my head
Reminding me that she is dead
Sweet, sweet K, she loved sweets
She had them everywhere, even around her feet!
Her colourful lights shone in her window, helping me sleep on
    sick nights
I could see them shining from her house, right opposite mine
We used to send messages through notes we threw
Connected by a string: *from me to you*
She had a swing in her room
I remember flying through the air, so freaking cool
Jumping onto her princess bed
I can still see her flowers in my head

Aunty, Where Are You?

Indigo-Rose Egundebi

The rooms are empty and silent. I can see boxes of all different soaps, handmade by her, ready to start the next big thing. The oxygen tanks to helped her breathe, fight against the horrible disease. Her son's bedroom right across from hers with dead fish in the tank, unfed. So again I ask, where are you? I remember seeing you in my back garden. You had a long braid hanging down from your head, the biggest smile and a yellow top with a black leather jacket. My eyes lit up when I saw you. It was a bright day, which made it even better. In a blink I am back to reality: a sad gloomy day with you away, but I know you are okay.

I love my Aunty Stacey. She will forever be in my heart with the wonderful memories that I could never ever forget.

My Unborn Brother

Mariam Daud

To my brother
I haven't met you yet
My brother
I can imagine your tiny feet
Kicking away in your own pitch-black space
My brother
The word feels weird on my tongue
But you are there
In our mother's uterus
I can't wait to meet you

Faduma

Stella Candido

I love walking into school and seeing her
She brings me joy just talking to her
Faduma is so kind
She is crazy, like
I love her as big as the whole universe
The thing is, I don't remember how we met
It's like we just started talking to each other
I remember her walking in, the first day of Year 7,
And BAM, we were besties; that can never be broken
I'm so glad we met
It brings me joy in my heart every single day

His Head Is a Mountain Waiting to Be Climbed

Tiago Costa

His heart is silver metal
His hairline is the Maccy Ds sign
His feet are two footballs scoring a goal
His hands are the net of the basketball hoop
Ready to catch

The Builder

Tiago Costa

An award given by the Queen, hung on the wall
No one to be seen in the room
His rusted safety helmet
Discarded on the bed that hasn't been slept in for years
No family pictures hanging on the wall
Discriminated against for being an immigrant
His science books open on the table
No cross on the wall
The music on the radio playing to no one

Whose Room?

Zayan Miah

A dark room with holes in the wall
On a shelf: a pair of Jordans and a dirty ball
A Quran on top of a cupboard
On the floor: an envelope of money
A plate of chicken on a bed as blue as the sky
A radio on the table, rusty
A picture of a family lost long ago
A TV that plays the weather in Moscow

PART THREE
OUR PLACES

Moon Poems

The moon is a portal to another dimension
The moon is hope in a world of despair
The moon is a CD
The moon is a grey stain
The moon is an uncoloured piece of paper

Princess Amosun

The moon is a light that shines
The moon is a bottle of sunscreen
The moon is a window blind
The moon is grey jeans
The moon is the non-identical twin of the sun

Zayan Miah

The moon is a chicken nugget
The moon is a cube full of pigs
The moon is an alien invasion
The moon is a cloud raining rats
The moon is a door to eternal life

Nesrin Osman

The moon is God's toy
The moon is a football
The moon is a chair
The moon is a beaker of light
The moon is a bumpy road

Tiago Costa

i) *OUR CITY, LONDON*

Where I Come From

Kamil Curtis

Where I come from it rains a lot / I hear fireworks a lot / it gets dark a lot / I don't get many sweets a lot / people die a lot / graves are made a lot / religion is a lot / we play basketball a lot / football is a lot / chicken is a lot / family is a lot / friends are a lot / love is a lot / school is a lot

London

Tiago Costa

The sun hidden by the clouds
The floor full of rubbish
The screaming in Brixton
The crowds of people getting onto the train
But then there's my family
Scattered around London
Like dominoes falling down

Where I Come From

Hamza Ali

Where I come from, it is always freezing
It's barely sunny, all cold
Men wear vests, even when it's raining
We buy fish and chips and eat all of it
The smell of Mum's cooking through the streets
When kids in school feel sad, they can't wait to go home
And that's my city
My city is not perfect, but I love it

Home Is

Hamza Ali

My home is London, mate.
London is sweet and caring.
London is sweet like candy.
Calm and nice like a hamster.
If home was a smell, it would be a bunch of flowers.
If home was a colour, it would be a rainbow.
If home was an object, it would be a luxury palace.
If home was a taste, it would be delicious, beautiful:
Mum's cooking flying through the whole house.

Where I Come From

Jahmarlley Bollers

It's sometimes cold
Sometimes hot
But I still love it
It's so easy to go places
On the buses
I really love London
I'm Jamaican
I'm Ghanaian
I'm still
A part of this community
People are hard workers
People are not always kind
Even if someone makes you feel sad
You shouldn't let that drag you down
Your family loves you still
We all love you
Deep in our hearts
And you will know
And you will find
A team mate

Home Is

Rosie Button

Home is where I was born. Grew up in this crazy place. It's fun but dangerous. I don't like it very much but here I am. It's beautiful and historic but some places are bad places to be. It's a well-known place that I'm happy to be in. If home was a smell, it would be vinegar. If home was a colour, it would be orange. If home was an object, it would be an old castle. If home was a taste, it would be fish and chips. If home was a feeling, it would be worry.

London Is a City of Happiness and Love

Felipe Silva

Smells of perfumes
Colours of grey and white like a rock
But home is hot and nice and warm
And it smells like the sea everywhere, all the time
It tastes like salt and fish
It is night, but it's still sunny out
In the morning it is the birds warbling
Kids can play out all by themselves

My School Life

Nasir Anderson St Aubyn

When I go to school, I see people running, talking and writing, and I hear laughing, shouting and screaming.

Sometimes I feel the paper and pen against my fingers, the hard table, the ink leaking and the glue smeared across my paper. I can always smell the food from the canteen. It feels like another home.

ii) *OTHER HOMES*

Home is Home

Faduma Adde

Somewhere there's
Love, harmony, peace
That's my home
Where everyone loves to pull a prank
Water balloons, shaving cream, we did it all
I cannot forget how amazingly we travelled
Going to Dubai was beautiful
The rivers flowed so swiftly
That's home to me

I Miss Home

Shelisha-Rayne Damsa

I whistle down the street the music that keeps me alive
Thoughts of home swallow me and keep me trapped
What's here for me?
Why can't I leave?
When will I see you again?
My heart starts hurting
Slowly, yet still too quick
I think of the desires that will never be fulfilled
The uniform I'll never wear
The things I'll never learn
The creatures I'll never meet
The friends I'll never make
I think of you and my heart strangles itself with longing
The nights we'll never spend together
The matches we'll never play on the team
The detentions you'll never bring me to
The place where I'm happy, I'll never see
Why must the journey be so difficult?
Why must I stay stuck in a world I want to leave?
Why must I think about a perfect world I'll never get to?
Was there a reason I discovered this world?
Was there a purpose?
Was it just the first blow, the first hit?
Was I just some toy in a cruel game?
Is that all I am meant to be?
    A dream, a hope, a fiction?
Am I forced to stay where my misery lies and forbidden to go
    to the land my heart loves?

I want to cry, just to unleash the tears fighting to be set free,
    but I can't
Because crying won't take me home
Nothing will...

Ivory Coast

Maferima Bamba

Where I come from
It's very hot
The roads are dirty brown dust
Nice people sell mangoes from the jungle
I eat the mangoes, juicy and sweet
Where I come from
The sea is full
Of crocodiles
Camouflaged as rocks
Where I come from
My grandma sits
On her chair
Outside in the shade
I say *assalamualaikum*

My Cookbook

Sashawnna Wilks

I walk into the kitchen and see my grandpa cooking
I start to help him with the fish
I hear the goat making sounds in the yard
While I start to mix
The fish starts to pop and sizzle
Like there is a firework in the sky
I start to jump and spin around with joy, and sniff
To smell the delicious food
I start to head to the living room
and I start to eat

My Winter

Sashawnna Wilks

I like the winter
I like hot chocolate
And snowy days and breezy nights
It gets cold and chilly and then I start
To cuddle and watch a film and drink
My warm hot chocolate
I cuddle and hug my dog
And think I hear people playing in the snow
I look outside to see a family
Making a snowman
I put on my jacket, my boots
My hat and my scarf
I jump and swirl and make
Snow angels
I pick up rocks, carrots and a scarf
To make my beautiful snowman
called Buttons
I start to play Catch and I am so happy
You are here
You are the best Christmas gift I've ever had
The Moon starts to move
I head to my cosy cabin
Start to get ready for bed
Dress my dog into an elf
Snuggle my pillow

The Clouds Are a Blanket to Keep the Sky Warm

Rosie Button

The winter is cold, cold like ice
The winter is beautiful, so very nice
Children playing in the snow
When it's time to go home they'll all say no
Snowflakes falling on people's noses
Doing snow angels in different poses
The night comes quick then it's time for bed
So let's lie down and rest our heads
Have a good winter's night
Everything will be all right

iii) *FINDING FREEDOM IN OUR SPACES*

Arriving at the Cafe

Yahya Rodani

Ready to unwind
The sunny breeze
Intercepted by the parasol
The conversations of families
Deciding which beverage
Will be consumed today
The smell of baking bread
Coffee beans mercilessly ground
The taste of contentment
The hiss of the fizz
Released from its eternal prison
Condensation cooling my hands
I grasp the bottle
The sun on my skin
Aiding my thirst
I drink the Coke
The Coke touches my throat
Hordes of memories
Flooding my mind
Reminiscences of the good times
All the good times

I Was There

Princess Amosun

I was welcomed by reuniting people: laughing, dancing,
    singing
And the birds whose chirps seemed to harmonise with them
The warm sun stroked my face, blinding me from seeing the
    beauty
But it was easily defeated by the shade of the leaves
Was I really there?
My face seemed to think so
People laughed, hugged, danced
Even the luscious green grass swayed along
A ripple disturbed the water in a nearby pond
And again
And again
And again
The sky poured down with misery, but the people only got
    happier
And so did I
I did not care
Because I was there
Finally

The World's Worries

Tiago Silva Jesus

Dogs barking
Families passing by
No more space
Babies crying
Loud screams
Infesting my ears
Horrors of the world
Zooming around
Uncomfortable
But just then
A sense of freedom comes
Space has been made
Music begins to play
Relax
The world's worries blocked off
Normality returns
Nothing left to do
Music dancing in my ears
Sun shining in my eyes
All is perfect
Finally

What a Wonderful Place to Be

Nesrin Osman

The burning-hot sun beaming down on the park
The wind, a passenger walking by, jealous of me
The flavour melting on my tongue
What a wonderful place to be
I can see where I want to be
I spy with my little eye
Something beginning with F
Family and friends sitting in the tree
Green grass, blue skies
I can see smoke flying soundlessly through the air
A picture appears: a familiar scene
People hiding behind the slide, waiting to be found
Line by line
A melody of hungry tummies
A day of fun
Not to be forgotten
A sense of happiness runs down my face
A taste of victory at my favourite game
Game over
A normal day
What a wonderful place to be

Taste of Victory

Tiago Costa

The taste of victory was delicate
Green beautiful grass getting swiftly battered by the ball
The ball slammed into the goal
Turning in the net
People screamed viciously like the wind
The only things you could smell were the sweat and polluted
    air
The taste of victory made us feel that the world was at our feet
The game was over
That beautiful game of football
And all we could see were the clear blue skies

iv) *WHAT IS HOME?*

Home is Home

Kamil Curtis

Home is home. Home is an endless portal to love and hope. Home with parents and family is a spectacular feeling of love and acceptance. Home is a stupendous world of love and joy. Home is another world to escape to. Home is breathtaking and phenomenal. Home is an abandoned world just waiting for family to heal it. Home is filled with astonishing memories. Home is like KFC chicken. Home is music to my ears.

Home

Ridwaan Isse

Home is the place where my culture feels welcome
Home is the checkpoint you can always come back to
Home is the safe place, where you don't need to steal

Spectacular food
Spectacular drinks
Sometimes I think Home is unreal

Be who you want to be
Do what you want to do
Home is the feeling you want to feel

You get your parents angry or upset
But Home is the place where love always heals

Home is the perfect place for me

Home

Shivani Clarke-Lewis

People say home is where the heart is
But that's not the case
Wherever my family is, that's definitely where I'll stay
The smell of my mum's cooking
Oh, so sweet and so good
The sound of my brothers laughing
If I could listen to it all day I would
Now, you might call me crazy but really you've just misunderstood
Because home isn't where the heart is
My family is where I'm stood

BIOGRAPHIES

FADUMA ADDE: My name's Faduma. I'm from Somalia but live in London. I like writing because I love to put my creativity on paper. It helps with my spelling too. I like writing about things I see. Poems are my favourite. They describe my wonderful memories the best.

HAMZA ALI: My name is Hamza. I live in London. I didn't always like school but the First Story programme was fun. I have always loved writing about my personal experiences at school and beyond. If you're stressed, I would recommend you try to overcome it, as I have learned that nothing is impossible. Overall, my experience with First Story has made me more confident in my writing ability.

PRINCESS AMOSUN: Princess is a student from England who loves creative writing as she is very creative and optimistic. She loves writing about the sunset, music and her family, as she's inspired by her little brother. She is striving to make more books in the future.

NASIR ANDERSON ST AUBYN: My name is Nasir and I like writing because it lets me explore my creativity and my imagination, and make stories, poems and all kinds of writing. I'm from Jamaica though I live in London and a fun fact about me is that I am a Virgo.

MAFERIMA BAMBA: Maferima is a young girl originating from Ivory Coast, but living in London. She loves Takis and chocolate. She lives with her parents, three brothers and a stepsister. She is very proud of the work she has produced with First Story.

JAHMARLLEY BOLLERS: Jahmarlley is a fantastic basketball player who loves to play football with his friends. He dreams of one day discovering a new planet.

ROSIE BUTTON: I'm Rosie and I really like acting, writing, music and doing drama at school. I live in England and it's a really good place to learn history. I love writing because it's a way to step away from your problems and let your brain lead you on.

STELLA CANDIDO: My name is Stella, I live in England but I'm Portuguese. I love writing because it's calming and helps me improve my English. I also love crocheting because it helps me express myself and is really creative. I also love playing with my dogs Ziggy and Nala.

SHIVANI CLARKE-LEWIS: Shivani is a Jamaican student from London who loves to write. She has two brothers named Shai and Shiloh, a loving, creative, inspiring mother (A) and a joyful, funny, loving Dad (C). She is very creative and talented, so when she heard she could write her own book she jumped at the offer.

TIAGO COSTA: My name is Tiago Costa. I go to Platanos College and I like writing about football.

KAMIL CURTIS: My name is Kamil. My past few weeks being a poem writer have been an extraordinary feeling. I feel more able to concentrate and able to do more in writing and English. Writing was my dream in primary school, where I read a lot of *Diary of a Wimpy Kid* books by Jeff Kinney. I felt like everything was set out for me: it was about my willpower so I just had to concentrate.

SHELISHA-RAYNE DAMSA: Shelisha is a Caribbean girl who lives in England. She loves writing fiction and fantasy stories as this allows her to think outside the box, not bound to the strings of reality. Shelisha is a huge Harry Potter fan. She loves reading, and personally prefers to write electronically.

MARIAM DAUD: Mariam is a young writer originating from Nigeria, but living in London. She loves writing because she loves reading and would like to share knowledge with others. She lives in a house with her parents, two sisters and a brother – soon to become two brothers. She loves rollerblading, gymnastics and doing well in school.

INDIGO-ROSE EGUNDEBI: Indigo-Rose is a student from London who is Jamaican and Nigerian. She loves to draw and write poems and fun stories to express her feelings. She loves her family and her little two-year-old rabbit. She loves being creative and would love to be a doctor when she is older.

RIDWAAN ISSE: My name is Ridwaan. My past few weeks as a writer have been wonderful. This has taught me to get better at poems and at writing in general. Growing up, becoming a writer was my dream. I read a lot of famous books by Roald Dahl, *Middle School* and *Diary of a Wimpy Kid*. I felt like something was stopping me, but I always had a little bit of endurance in me, and that's how I became more focused on writing. And here I am!

ZAYAN MIAH: Zayan loves football and maths. He aspires to be the first person in his family to become a doctor.

NESRIN OSMAN: Hi. My name is Nesrin and I am a student at Platanos College. My passion is poetry. My artistic mind spills onto the page and magically creates a poem. I live in London, a populated city. I was inspired by my lovely English teacher, Ms O'Connell.

KARINA RIBEIRO SANCHES: Karina is a Portuguese student who was born and raised in London. She loves to write as it helps distract her from her younger brothers' antics. She loves to write about different fantasy worlds made up in her mind. She writes to give others a story to read, while adding in real-world problems so as to not stray far from reality. She loves her cats Milo and Onyx, drawing and animating, and her family and friends – even those who are not too close to home.

YAHYA RODANI: Hello. My name is Yahya. I live in London but am from Morocco. I like eating Oreos and writing about food.

ISRAE SEHIMI: I'm Israe and I like drama and inspiring people. I am from Morocco and I really like it there. I like writing because it helps me to escape from reality, and focus.

FELIPE SILVA: My name is Filipe. In my language, my name is written Felipe. My home is Portugal. It is hot and warm, but I came to London when I was two. When I first came to London, I was not a big fan of the cold, but since living here I am more used to it now. Being part of the First Story programme has been fun and enjoyable.

TIAGO SILVA JESUS: Hello. My name is Tiago Silva Jesus. I like playing with my cat and drinking coffee. I'm from Portugal and music inspires me to think.

SASHAWNNA WILKS: Sashawnna is a Caribbean girl who like animals and cooking. She likes helping her family do farming. Her dream job is to be a singer or a runner. She likes to write poems and stories too. Her friends motivate her to be the best self that she can be. She hopes one day you will achieve your dreams too.

Acknowledgements

Melanie Curtis at Avon DataSet for her overwhelming support for First Story, and for giving her time in typesetting this anthology.

Kirsten Irving for copy-editing and Ingrid Wassenaar for proofreading this anthology.

Jennifer Hines for designing the cover of this anthology.

Foysal Ali at Aquatint for printing this anthology at a discounted rate.

Thanks to our funders:
Jane & Peter Aitken, Amazon Literary Partnership, Authors' Licensing & Collecting Society, Arts Council England, Blue Thread, Fiona Byrd, Charlotte Aitken Trust, Drapers' Charitable Fund, Garfield Weston Foundation, Goldsmiths' Company Charity, John Lyon's Charity, John R Murray Charitable Trust, Julia and Hans Rausing Trust, Man Charitable Trust, Mercers' Company Charity, Paul Hamlyn Foundation, teamArchie, Wellington Management UK Foundation, the Friends of First Story and our regular supporters, individual donors, community fundraisers and those supporters who choose to remain anonymous.

Pro bono supporters and delivery partners including:

Arvon Foundation, BBC Teach, British Library, Cambridge University, Centre for Literacy in Primary Education, English and Media Centre, Forward Arts Foundation, Goldsmiths, University of London, Hachette, Manchester Metropolitan University, National Literacy Trust, Manchester and Nottingham UNESCO Cities of Literature, Nottingham Trent University, Penguin Random House, Rathbones Folio Prize, University of Greenwich, University of Huddersfield, University of Hull, University of Leicester, University of Manchester and University of Nottingham.

Most importantly, we would like to thank the students, teachers and writers who have worked so hard to make First Story a success this year, as well as the many individuals and organisations (including those we may have omitted to name) who have generously given their time, support and advice.